The Hour of the Frog

For little Lewis. TWJ
For my aunt, Helen. C O'N

Text copyright © 1989 Tim Wynne-Jones
Illustrations copyright © 1989 Catharine O'Neill

A Groundwood Book
Douglas & McIntyre Ltd.
26 Lennox Street
Toronto, Canada M6G 1J4

Canadian Cataloguing in Publication Data

Wynne-Jones, Tim
  The hour of the frog
ISBN 0-88899-096-0

I. O'Neill, Catharine. II. Title

PS8595.Y66H68 1989 jC813'.54 C89-093425-8
PZ7.W96Ho 1989

Designed and lettered by Catharine O'Neill
Printed and bound in Hong Kong by
Everbest Printing Co., Ltd.

The Hour of the Frog

Written by

Tim Wynne-Jones

Illustrated by

Catharine O'Neill

a Groundwood Book

DOUGLAS & McINTYRE
VANCOUVER   TORONTO

It is night.

Fred and Dreadnought are asleep.

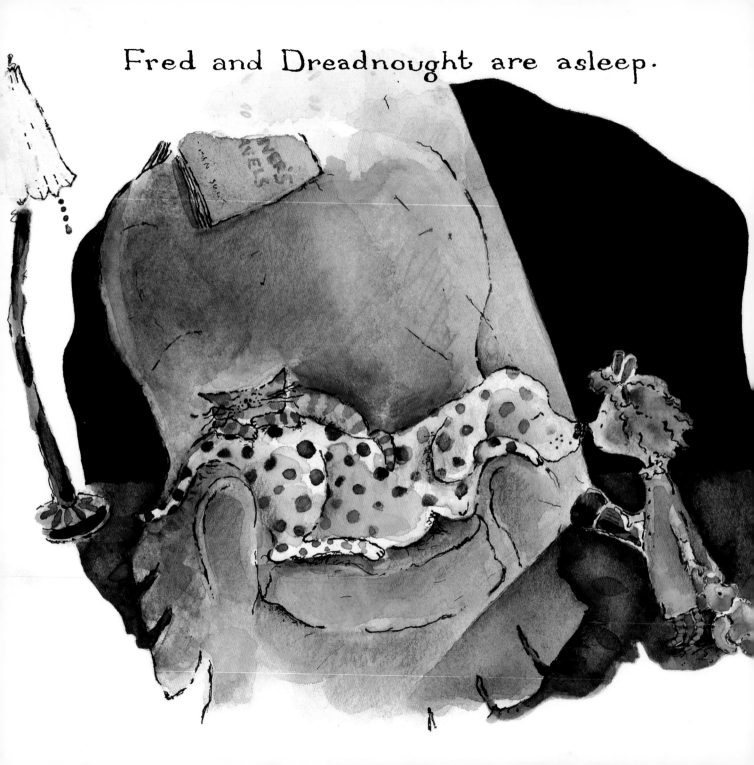

Mum and Dad are asleep.

Thunder and Frisco and Lyle
are asleep.

But not me.

It is the Hour of the Frog.

What's that ?

DRIP

DRIP

DRIP

Thlump !

Out of his slimy
hole in the wall...

Thlump.   Thlump.
        Thlump.

He crosses the living room floor.
Thlippety - thlump. Thlippety - thlump.
Thlippety - thlop - thlop. Thlippety - thlump,

to dance
in his frog suit
up and down
the front hall.

Then off to...

the kitchen.

What's that!
The knife in the pickle jar.
Frog is making a sandwich.
Eggs and mayo, peanut butter, onions and

Flies !

On a sticky bun.
The Hour of the Frog snack.

Thlump. Slurp. Bump.
He's heading my way.
I pull the covers up over my head.

Thlump.   Thlump.
He's at the foot of the stairs.
The smell of pickle juice floats up
in the air and through my open door.

I hide under the covers.
I try to keep quiet but...
Thlump. Bump.
I can't stop myself.
"Oh no," says I. "Oh, woe is me."

And there
in the gloom
of the landing
Frog stops in his slimy tracks.
"Oh, woe?" says he.
"Ho, ho," says he.
"You don't scare me."

"Oh no?" says I,
rising way up high. Then
"Go!" I cry.

And Froggy leaps
almost out of his skin
onto the banister.

Then thlippety-thlump. I hear Frog jump
a-wooing all the way
back to his slimy hole in the wall.

Back to the swamp.
SPLAASH! Like every night.

But I still can't sleep.

So I turn my mind to breakfast.

French toast and butter...Zzz...
Maple syrup... and...

Flies !